A Gift For:

_____

From:

_____

Editor: Emily Osborn
Art Director: Jan Mastin
Production Designer: Dan Horton

ISBN: 978-1-59530-546-6
VTD5061

Printed and bound in China
AUG12

Cupig's Shuffle

Written by Erin Canty
Illustrated by Pete Whitehead

Hallmark
gift books

It's been said that the rare and majestic flying pig is best known for its ability to spread love and joy with the fling of an arrow. *Boom! Zip! Pow!* –Happiness to all the land.

And while the gift of archery comes naturally to most flying pigs, this was not the case for Cupig.

His arrows went left. His arrows went right. They went upward and backward, downward and frontward, but never where he wanted them to go.

For as hard as he tried, little Cupig was not a strong archer . . . especially next to the Belchingham brothers, Hank, Tank, and Fitzhubert.

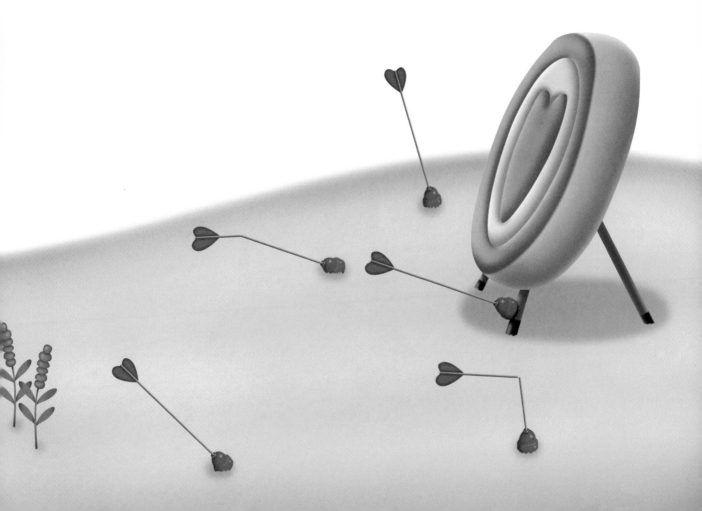

The Belchingham brothers were strong, fast, and big, big meanies.

"You're just a baby, Cupig!" said Hank.

"Yeah, you'll never hit targets like us!" said Tank.

"I'm all outta cheese!" said Fitzhubert.

Cupig was determined to get better, so every day he practiced shooting arrows. And though he improved, he was still no match for those Belchingham brothers.

But, despite his poor archery skills, Cupig knew there was something only *he* could do, something that made him a unique and special pig. Cupig loved to dance.

He wiggled. He jiggled. He shimmied and shook. Where there was music there was Cupig, right in the middle of it, curly tail and all.

He was good, excellent even, but not everyone appreciated his talent.

"Cut it out!" said Tank.

"Whatcha doin' that for?" asked Hank.

"Who moved the pretzels?" asked Fitzhubert.

"Don't listen to them, Cupig," said his mother.
"Just be yourself. You're one special pig." And he was.

So he practiced and he danced.
Then he danced and he practiced.
He did this each and every day.
And before he knew it, it was
Valentine's Day.

As far as days of significance for flying pigs go, Valentine's Day is at the top of the list. Hank, Tank, and Fitzhubert zoomed into the sky launching their arrows. An overwhelming feeling of love filled the air.

Cupig shot his arrows, too, but they didn't hit much; a tree, a car, and the flagpole outside the big brick schoolhouse. He was retrieving his arrows when the Belchingham brothers found him.

"We already visited the school, Silly!" said Hank.

"Yeah, those arrows should be working their magic any minute," said Tank.

"Got any candy?" asked Fitzhubert.

Cupig sighed. This was his time to shine, and he wasn't spreading any love at all. Maybe the Belchingham brothers were right; maybe he wasn't so special after all.

But then he heard something. His ears perked up. "Is that what I think it is?" he thought.

He zipped past the Belchingham brothers and followed the sound into the school.
His curly tail began to twitch. Yes, it was music!

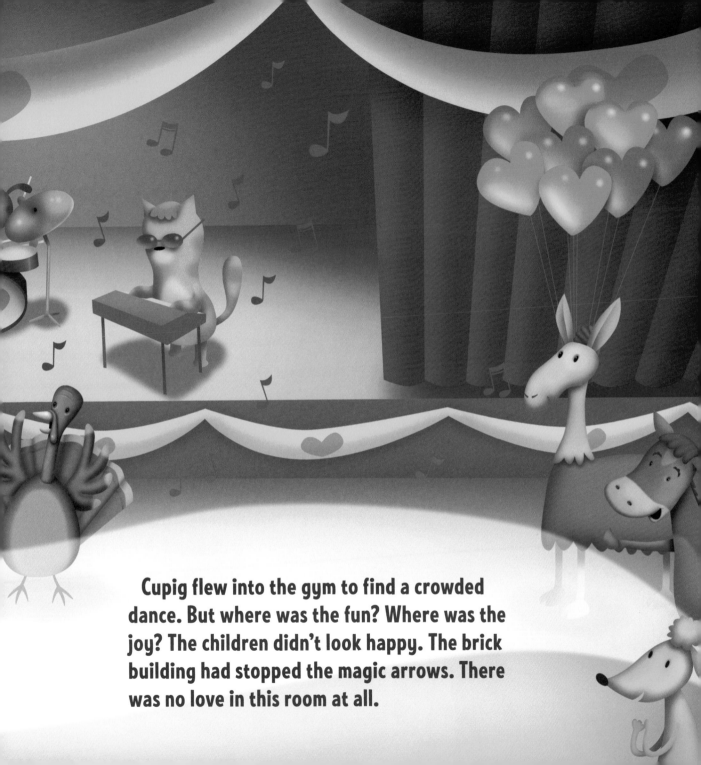

Cupig flew into the gym to find a crowded dance. But where was the fun? Where was the joy? The children didn't look happy. The brick building had stopped the magic arrows. There was no love in this room at all.

But Cupig knew just what to do.
He walked to the center of the gym,
then took a deep breath . . .

. . . and he danced, and danced, and danced.
Before he knew it, the children were dancing, too!

They were laughing! They were smiling! They were having fun! Cupig had saved the day!

Hearing all the commotion, even the Belchingham
brothers couldn't resist jumping in.
"Way to go, Cupig!" said Hank.
"Let's boogie!" said Tank.
"Do I smell peanut butter?" asked Fitzhubert.

Cupig did it! He'd found a new way to spread joy and love. And best of all, he did it by being himself. Cupig looked forward to being himself more often . . . and dancing to spread the love.

Have you enjoyed dancing with Cupig?
We would love to hear from you.

Please send your comments to:
Hallmark Book Feedback
P.O. Box 419034
Mail Drop 215
Kansas City, MO 64141

Or e-mail us at:
booknotes@hallmark.com